This Orchard
book belongs to

....

....

....

To Andrea, who keeps
me on my toes – J.J.

For little Rosie – G.P-R.

ORCHARD BOOKS

First published in Great Britain in 2010 by Orchard Books
This edition published in 2011 by The Watts Publishing Group

Text © Julia Jarman, 2010
Illustrations © Guy Parker-Rees, 2010

The moral rights of the author and illustrator have been asserted.

A CIP catalogue record for this book is available from the British Library.

ISBN 978 1 40834 676 1

Printed and bound in China

Orchard Books
An imprint of Hachette Children's Group
Part of The Watts Publishing Group Limited
Carmelite House, 50 Victoria Embankment
London EC4Y 0DZ

An Hachette UK Company
www.hachette.co.uk

www.hachettechildrens.co.uk

Julia Jarman Guy Parker-Rees

ANTS
IN YOUR
PANTS!

ORCHARD

Leopard was having a party.

"But only
for really
cool dudes.

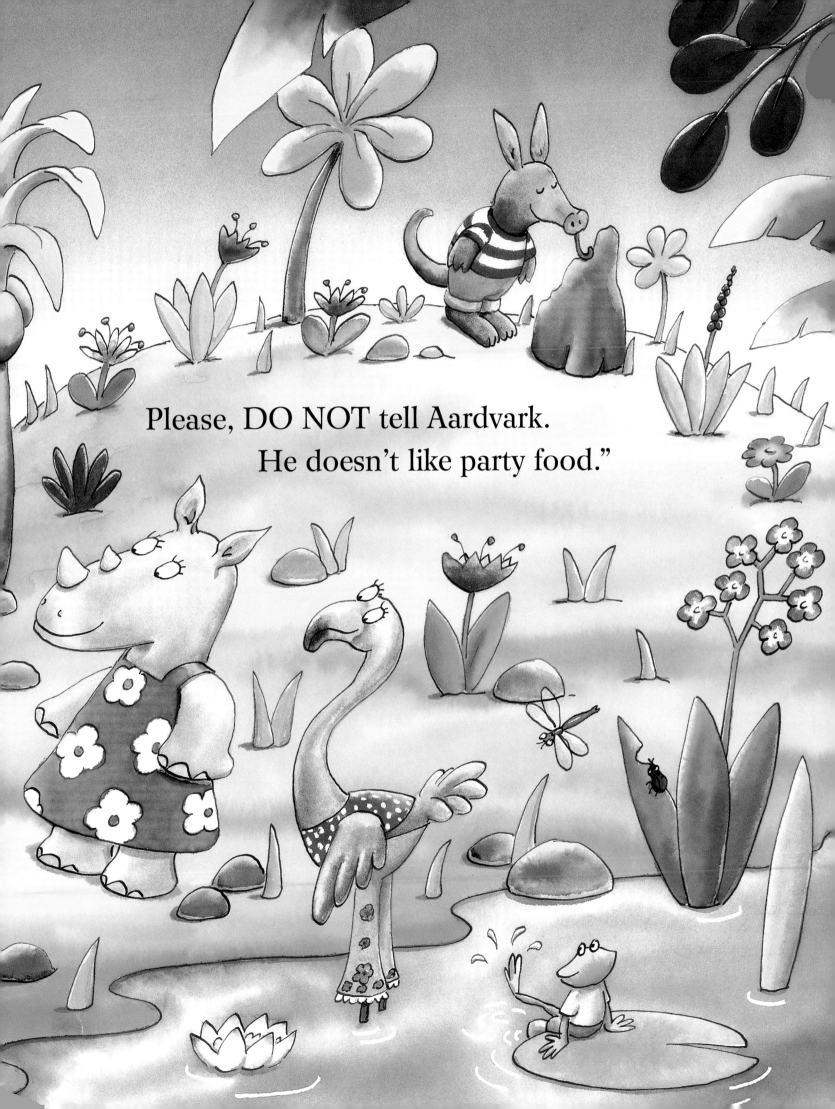

Please, DO NOT tell Aardvark.
He doesn't like party food."

Leopard got ever so anxious
About the food and the drink.

"What about my
birthday cake?

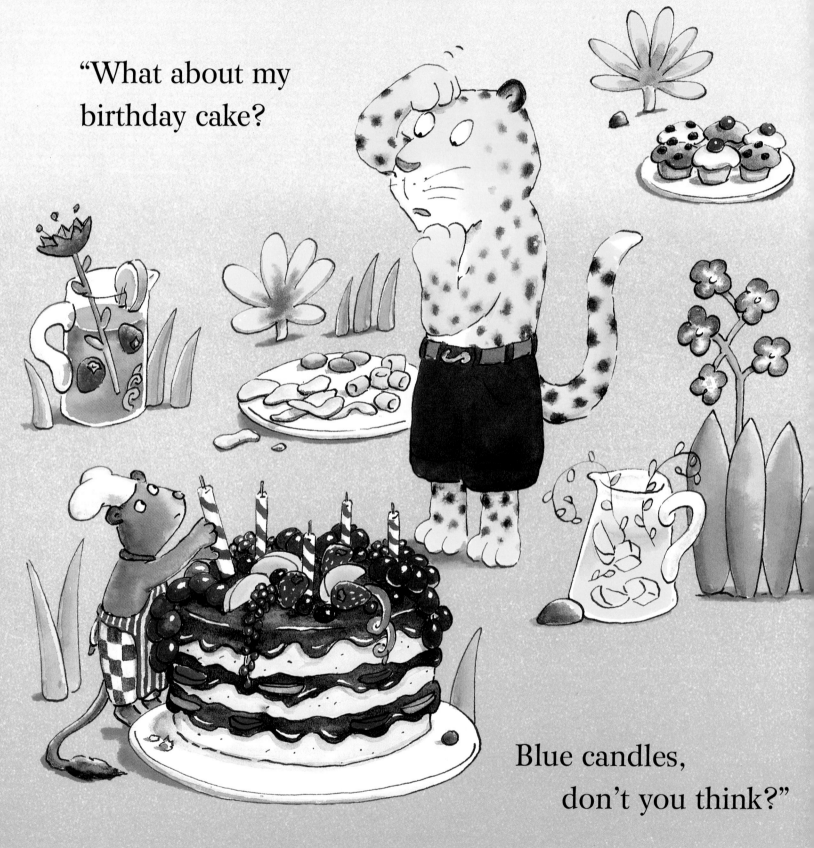

Blue candles,
don't you think?"

"But don't, do NOT, tell Aardvark.
He really mustn't know.
He only eats ants and cucumbers . . .

And he slurps
them down
in one go!"

Now Aardvark wasn't that bothered
(And he *did* hear the word going round),

But he liked to roam . . .

or play at home . . .

With Big Sis under the ground.

But *someone* was *very* offended
Not to get one of
Leopard's invites.

Big Ant hurried home
and got on the phone, "There's a party
at Leopard's tonight."

Now ants really like parties.
They enjoy a good bop with their chums.

They like party food

and games that are rude –

Like *Who Can Bite
the Most Bums?*

The party guests started arriving,
Unaware of Big Ant's secret plot:

"First get to Leopard's party, then find yourself a bot."

The guests didn't hear the order
To all the other cross ants . . .

"Wait until everyone's eating,
Then start playing ANTS IN YOUR PANTS!"

"Let's party!" Leopard said loudly,
And everyone started to sing.

Nobody saw
     the chomping jaws
          Of ants getting ready to sting!

Then Croc cried, "Can we start eating? I want some lollies on sticks!"

"Me too! Me too!" cried Cockatoo.

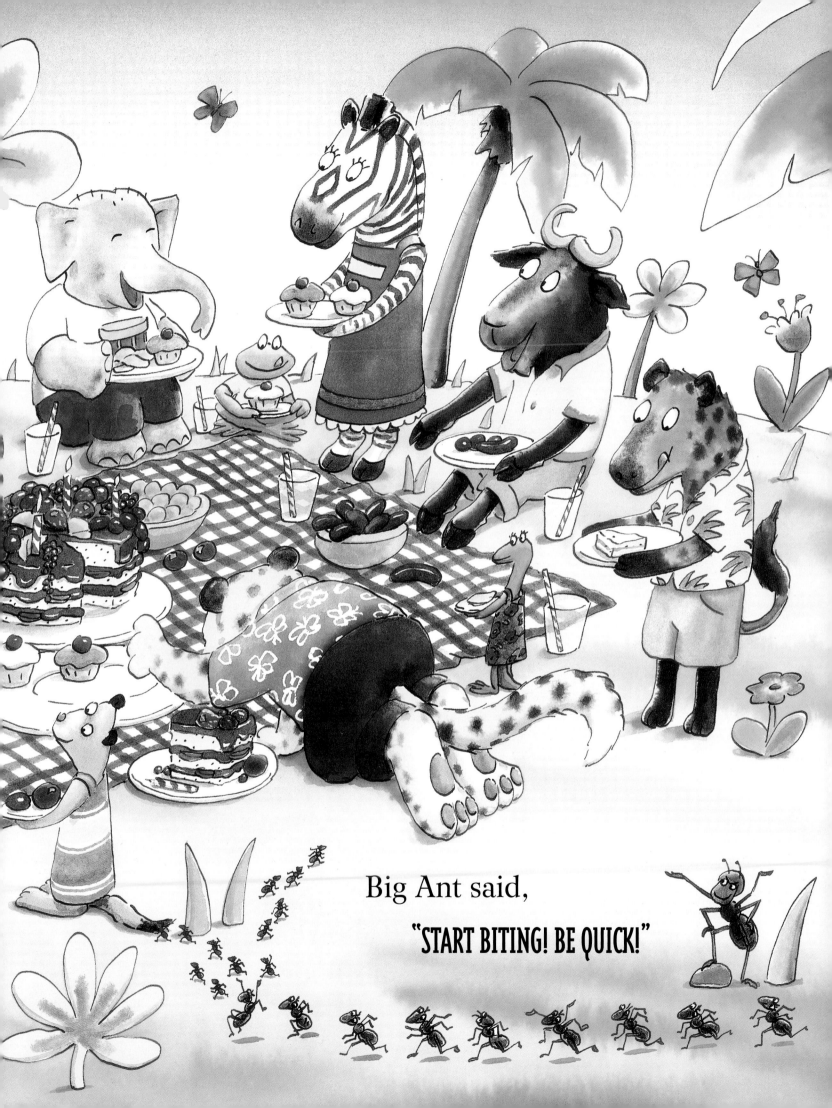

Big Ant said,

"START BITING! BE QUICK!"

Suddenly Leopard was leaping
Ever so high in the air,

Tearing off
his best trousers

And showing
his underwear!

Soon all the guests were jumping,
Throwing their pants in the air,

Trying to stop
those naughty ants –

Some of their
bottoms were
bare!

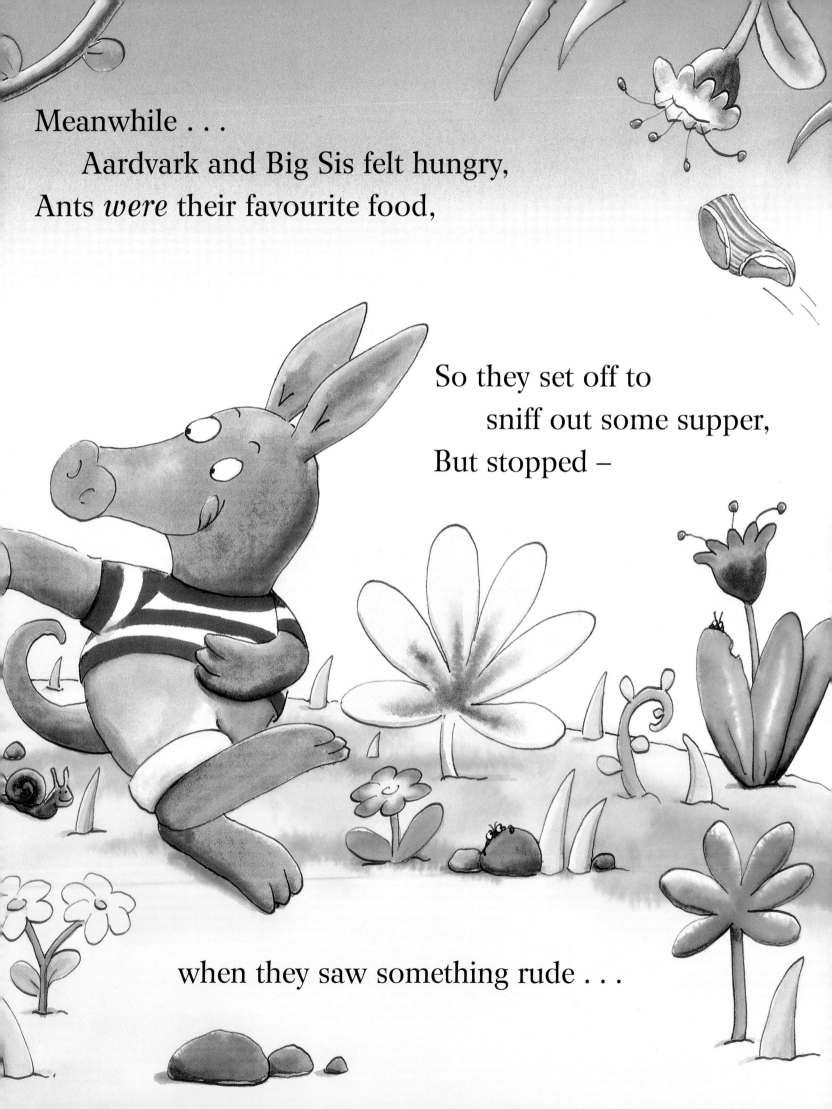

Meanwhile . . .
    Aardvark and Big Sis felt hungry,
Ants *were* their favourite food,

So they set off to
    sniff out some supper,
But stopped –

when they saw something rude . . .

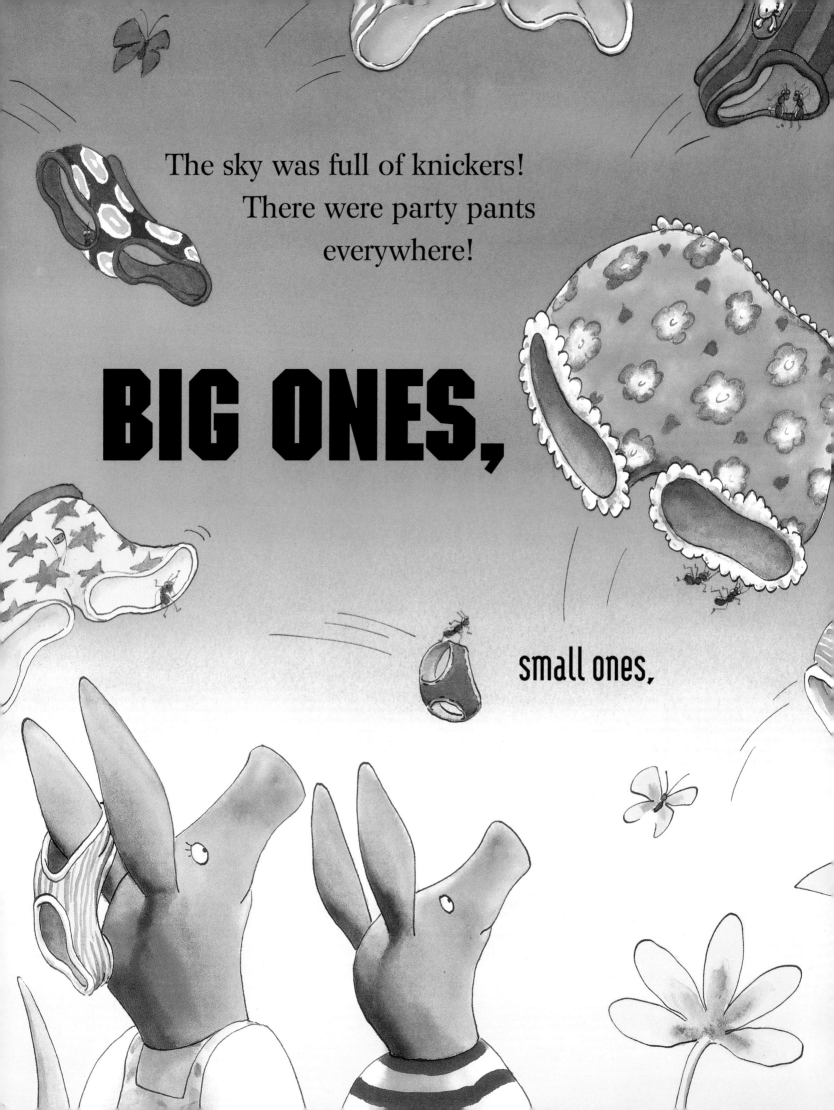

The sky was full of knickers!
There were party pants
everywhere!

BIG ONES,

small ones,

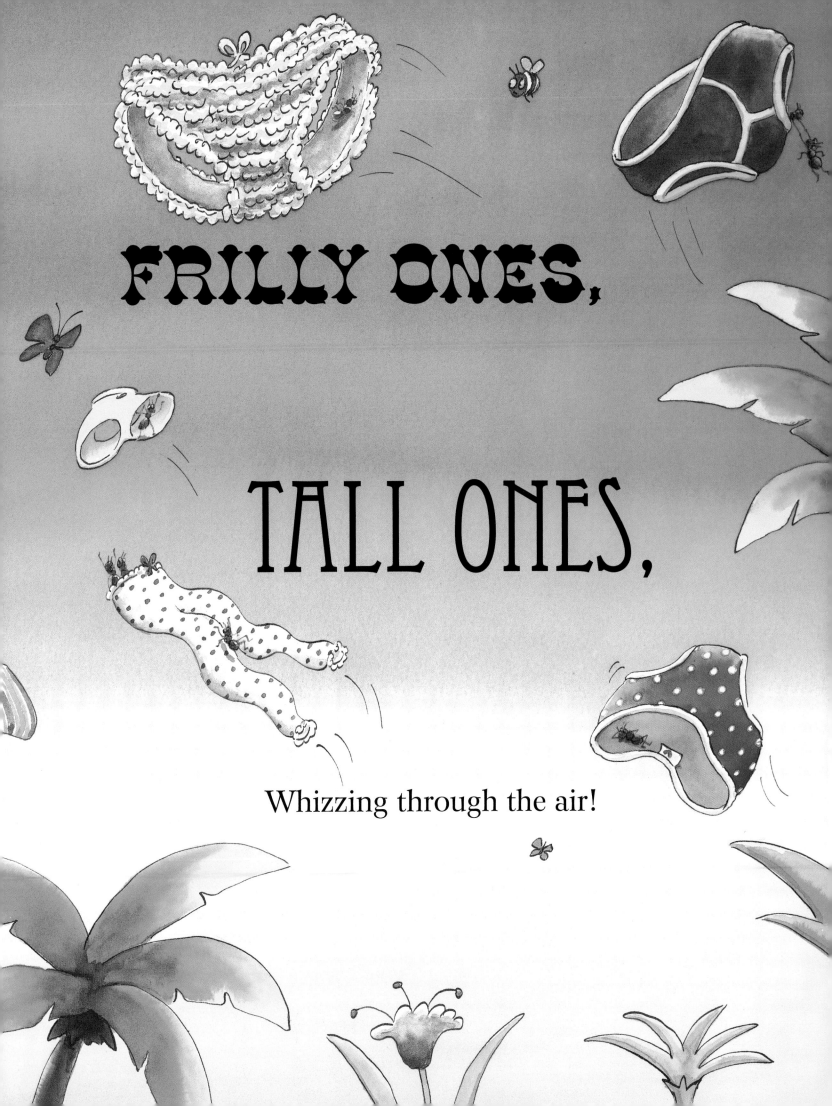

FRILLY ONES,

TALL ONES,

Whizzing through the air!

"What *is* going on?" asked Big Sis,
Watching Elephant hop.

"Oh, it's the party," said Aardvark.
"They're having
a bit of a bop."

"We didn't get an invite,
But while we're here let's feast."

He stuck out his tongue,

"Yummy,
yum,
yum!"

"Cor! Thanks!"
sighed Wilderbeest.

"Why *didn't* you invite us?"
Said Aardvark, wrinkling his snout.
"I'm really sorry," said Leopard.
"I was wrong to leave you out."

"I'll tell you something though,"
he smiled,
As Big Sis licked his ear.

"Now, you'll *both* be invited
To my party every year!"